April & Mae
and the
Talent Show

April & Mae

and the

Talent Show

THE WEDNESDAY BOOK

MEGAN DOWD LAMBERT

Illustrated by BRIANA DENGOUE

ini Charlesbridge

To my extended Lambert family, with thanks for
a lifetime of annual family-reunion talent shows,
and especially to cousins Violet and Eva—M. D. L.

To my daughter, Bellarose—B. D.

Published by Charlesbridge
9 Galen Street, Watertown, MA 02472 • (617) 926-0329 • www.charlesbridge.com

Library of Congress Cataloging-in-Publication Data
Names: Lambert, Megan Dowd, author. | Dengoue, Briana, illustrator.
Title: April & Mae and the talent show: the Wednesday book / Megan Dowd
    Lambert; illustrated by Briana Dengoue.
Other titles: April and Mae and the talent show
Description: Watertown. MA: Charlesbridge, 2022. | Series: Every day with
    April & Mae | Audience: Ages 5–8. | Summary: "April and Mae are best friends
    (and so are their pets). When April freezes onstage during the talent show,
    Mae knows just how to help."—Provided by publisher.
Identifiers: LCCN 2020050992 (print) | LCCN 2020050993 (ebook) |
ISBN 9781623542610 (hardcover) | ISBN 9781632898500 (ebook)
Subjects: LCSH: Talent shows—Juvenile fiction. | Stage fright—Juvenile fiction. |
    Best friends—Juvenile fiction. | Pets—Juvenile fiction. | CYAC: Talent shows—
    Fiction. | Bashfulness—Fiction. | Best friends—Fiction. | Friendship—Fiction. |
    Pets—Fiction.
Classification: LCC PZ7.1.L26 Ao 2022 (print) | LCC PZ7.1.L26 (ebook) |
    DDC 813.6 [E]—dc23
LC record available at https://lccn.loc.gov/2020050992
LC ebook record available at https://lccn.loc.gov/2020050993

Printed in China
(hc) 10 9 8 7 6 5 4 3 2 1

Illustrations done in Photoshop
Illustrations line art finalized by Gisela Bohórquez
Illustrations colorized by Collaborate
Display type set in Jacoby by Adobe
Text type set in Grenadine by Markanna Studios Inc.
Color separations and printing by 1010 Printing International Limited
    in Huizhou, Guangdong, China
Production supervision by Jennifer Most Delaney
Designed by Cathleen Schaad

April and Mae
have many talents.

April makes music.
Mae makes art.
Mae is shy.
April is not.
April is bold.
Mae is not.

But April and Mae are friends.
Best friends.
And their pets
are best friends, too.

On Wednesdays,
April and Mae take classes.
April takes music class.
Mae takes art class.
It is fun!

One Wednesday,
they find out
about a talent show.
It will be at the park.
It will help pay for new books
for the library.

TALENT SHOW
TO HELP THE
LIBRARY!

DOG TRAINING

TEA PARTY TREATS

CAT CARE

SCARY STORIES

SOCCER

ALL ABOUT ART

VOLUNTEERS NEEDED

"Look, Mae!" says April.
"We can be in a talent show
to help the library."
"That is a nice idea," says Mae.
"You do not look happy,"
says April.

"I want to help," says Mae.
"But I do not want
 to be in a talent show."
"But you are very talented,"
 says April.
"I am also very shy," says Mae.
"You are a great artist," says April.
 Mae's eyes get big.
"I will *not* draw onstage!" says Mae.

"No," says April.

"You can draw posters."

"To help sell tickets?" asks Mae.

"Yes!" says April.

"Everyone will look at the posters
and not at me," says Mae.

"Yes!" says April.

Mae's smile gets big.

"I can make treats for
a bake sale, too," says Mae.

"That is a nice idea," says April.

Mae makes lots of posters.
April puts them up
all over town.
"Your posters are great," says April.
"I hope a big crowd comes,"
says Mae.
"Me, too," says April.

On talent show day,
April and Mae go to the park.
Mae brings her cat in a basket.
April brings her dog on a leash.
They help set up.
Mae puts out her treats.
"You made *lots* of treats!" says April.
"Try one," says Mae.
"Yum!" says April.

April and Mae put out chairs.
"My posters helped sell
lots of tickets," says Mae.
April is happy for Mae.

Mae looks at the line of people.
"That is a *long* line," says April.
"Are you feeling shy?" asks Mae.
"No," says April.

But April is not sure about that.

"Will you sit in front?" asks April.

"Yes," says Mae.

"Will you hold my dog's leash?"
 asks April.

"Yes," says Mae.

"Will you smile and clap?"
 asks April.

"Yes," says Mae.

 Then Mae says,

"It's OK if you feel shy, April."

"I do not feel shy," says April.

 But Mae is not sure about that.

Everyone comes
into the park.
Many people buy treats.
The big crowd sits in the chairs.
Mae sits up front
with her cat.
She holds April's dog's leash.

April walks onto the stage.
She sees everyone
sitting in the chairs.
She hears everyone
munching their treats.
She feels her belly flop.
She wishes
she had not eaten a treat.

She sits on the bench.
She puts her hands on the keys.
She does not play.

Someone sneezes.
April looks at Mae.
Mae smiles.
April still does not play.

Someone coughs.
April's dog wags his tail.
Mae smiles a bigger smile.
But April cannot play.
April feels shy!

Mae stands up.
She lets go of April's dog's leash.
Mae needs to be bold
for her friend.
Mae claps for April.

April closes her eyes.

Mae cheers for April.
"Yay, April!" she calls.

Then Mae's cat sees a bird.
"Meow!"

Mae's cat chases the bird.
He runs onstage.
"Woof!" barks April's dog.
He chases Mae's cat.

Plink! Plink! Plink!
Mae's cat jumps on the piano.

Mae claps louder.
"Hooray for my cat!" she calls.
Now everyone claps.

Plink! Plink! Plink!

Someone laughs.

Plink! Plink! Plink!

Everyone laughs.

Mae's cat jumps down.
April laughs now, too.
She cannot let Mae's cat
steal the show.
She is April!
She is bold!
She will play!
April puts her hands on the keys.

April plays.
She plays
and plays.
Everyone claps to the beat.

April's song is over.
She takes a bow.
She does not feel shy.
She feels happy.
Mae is happy for April.

"You did it, April!" says Mae.
"*We* did it, Mae," says April.
"Yes, my posters helped
   get a big crowd," says Mae.

"And your cat helped me
play for them," says April.
"He is very talented," says Mae.
"Just like us."

"I felt shy, just like you," says April.
"Everyone feels shy sometimes,"
says Mae.
"I did not know that," says April.
"I did not know I could be bold
and cheer so loud," says Mae.
"Everyone looked at you," says April.
"I know!" says Mae.

The friends walk home.
"I am sorry I dropped your dog's
   leash," says Mae.
"It's OK," says April.
"He helped your cat play piano."
"And we all helped get more books
   for the library," says Mae.
"We did!" says April.

"Goodbye," says Mae.
"See you tomorrow," says April.

And goodbye to you, too.